Libby
the Story-Writing Fairy

by Daisy Meadows

ORCHARD

www.rainbowmagic.co.uk

The Fairyland Palace

Sara Sketchley's house

Bridge

Maze

Park

Rainspell Island

Cary's Jewellery Shop

Beach and Promenade

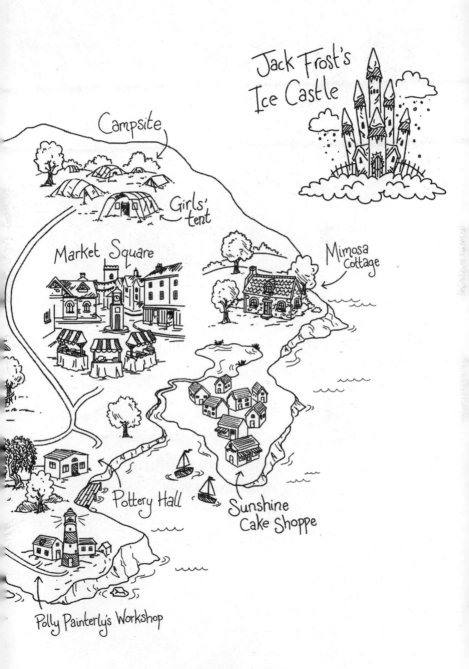

Jack Frost's
Ice Castle

Campsite

Girls'
tent

Mimosa
Cottage

Market Square

Pottery Hall

Sunshine
Cake Shoppe

Polly Painterly's Workshop

Jack Frost's Spell

I'm a wonderful painter, you must have heard of me,
Marvel at my amazing artistic ability!
With palette, brush and paints in hand,
I'll be the most famous artist in the land!

The Magical Crafts Fairies can't stop me,
I'll steal their magic and then you'll see
That everyone, whatever the cost,
Will want a painting by Jack Frost!

Contents

Stories in a Spin

"I wish I could paint like you, Kirsty!" Rachel said, holding up her friend's picture so she could admire it. The two girls had attended a painting workshop at Rainspell Lighthouse the day before. "Mum, don't you think this painting is really good?"

Mrs Walker was sitting in a deckchair outside their tent, soaking up the sunshine. She smiled and nodded. "You're very talented, Kirsty," Mrs Walker declared, taking the canvas to have a closer look. "You've got Rachel's hair and eye colour exactly right, and that rainbow arching over her head looks beautiful."

"Thanks!" Kirsty laughed. "Artie Johnson, the Crafts Week organiser, told me I should enter it in the competition tomorrow."

"And she also said you needed to choose a title for the picture," Rachel reminded her.

"How about *Rachel Under a Rainbow?*" suggested Mr Walker. He was also seated outside the tent, book in hand. "Perfect!" said Kirsty, and Rachel grinned. The girls were spending the spring holiday on Rainspell Island with their parents, and they were having the best time ever. It was Crafts Week on Rainspell and every day there were different activities for the girls to try. The Tates were staying in a B&B in the village while the Walkers had rented a large tent on the campsite. Rachel and

Kirsty were enjoying taking it in turns to spend one night at the B&B, then the next at the campsite.

"Whenever I look at your painting, it always reminds me of when we met the Rainbow Fairies right here on Rainspell Island, Kirsty," Rachel whispered.

"Me, too," Kirsty whispered back. "I'll never forget our very first fairy adventure!"

"Girls, are you off to a Crafts Week workshop today?" called Mrs Walker.

"Yes, Mum, but we haven't decided which one yet," Rachel replied.

"I think there might be a story-writing workshop this morning," Kirsty said. "One of the other students at the painting class mentioned it yesterday."

"Maybe we could write a story about

the Rainbow Fairies and take it along to the workshop," Rachel whispered. "No one would ever guess it was true!"

"Great idea," Kirsty agreed.

The girls sat on the grass with pens and paper and began to scribble down their ideas.

"It all started when we both came to Rainspell on holiday and I met you on the boat," Rachel murmured.

"I thought we met in the village?" Kirsty said, frowning.

Rachel thought for a moment and shook her head. "No, I don't think so," she replied. "Then we rescued Fern the Green Fairy from the pot of gold."

"But we saw the rainbow first," Kirsty reminded her.

Rachel felt very confused. "Did we?" she asked. "I don't remember that."

"Wasn't it Ruby the Red Fairy we rescued from the pot?" Kirsty wondered. "Or was it Saffron the Yellow Fairy?"

The girls stared doubtfully at each other. Suddenly Mr Walker groaned in disgust and threw his book down.

"This story doesn't make sense!" he sighed. "It's about a cowboy in the Wild West and it was brilliant, really gripping. Well, the cowboy's just taken off in a spaceship. How ridiculous!"

"Oh!" Kirsty's eyes grew round. "Rachel, I know what's happening and why the stories are going all wrong. It's because of Jack Frost!"

When Rachel and Kirsty arrived on Rainspell, they'd been greeted by Kayla the Pottery Fairy, one of the seven Magical Crafts Fairies. Kayla had explained that not only was it Crafts Week on Rainspell, it was Magical Crafts Week in Fairyland, too, and she'd invited the girls to join them for the opening ceremony of this very special occasion. All the fairies were excited because King Oberon and Queen Titania would be choosing the best crafts items to display in their royal palace.

But as Rachel and Kirsty watched Queen Titania's opening speech, Jack Frost and his goblins had run riot, tossing paint-filled balloons into the horrified crowd. The Magical Crafts Fairies and Queen Titania herself had been splattered with bright green paint, and in the total chaos and confusion, Jack Frost and his goblins snatched the Magical Crafts Fairies' special objects for themselves.

"I am the best artist ever and no one else is allowed to be better than me!" Jack Frost had declared. Then, with one flick of his wand, he'd conjured up a magical ice bolt that swept himself and his goblins away to the human world, taking the magical objects with them. With the help of the Magical Crafts Fairies, Kirsty and Rachel had set about finding as many of the special objects as they could. Both girls were determined to make sure that crafts everywhere, whether in the human or the fairy worlds, would still be fun and enjoyable and not spoilt by Jack Frost's selfish behaviour.

"Yes, Libby the Story-Writing Fairy's magical object is still missing," Rachel murmured. "That's why our stories are all jumbled up."

Kirsty bit her lip anxiously. "Rachel, wouldn't it be *terrible* if stories everywhere were just muddled-up nonsense?" she cried. "We'd never be able to read our favourite books again!"

"I know," Rachel sighed. "Jack Frost has really gone and done it this time!"

"Let's look at the Crafts Week brochure and find out more about the story-writing workshop," suggested Kirsty.

The girls dashed into the tent and found the brochure. Rachel flipped through it.

"Here it is," she announced. "*Story-writing workshop in the park, led by best-selling children's author, Poppy Fields.*"

"Poppy Fields!" Kirsty exclaimed, thrilled. "Rachel, she's one of our favourite writers!"

"I know!" Rachel agreed enthusiastically, "She's amazing. I *love* the way she retells old fairytales. I have all her books."

"Me, too," said Kirsty, a big grin on her face. "Let's head over to the park now. Maybe Poppy Fields herself will be able to help us with our story!"

Fairytale Fiasco!

The girls hurried off to the park in the nearby village. When they arrived, they followed the signs and saw a group of children seated on picnic rugs near the playground, waiting for the story-writing workshop to start. A dark-haired woman with a smiley face was perched on a beanbag in front of them, a pile of books by her side.

"Look, Kirsty," Rachel whispered excitedly as they found a space to sit. "That's Poppy Fields – I recognise her from the photo on her books!"

Kirsty and Rachel were both delighted when Poppy grinned at them in a very friendly way. "Welcome, girls," she called. "You're just in time. Hello, everyone, and welcome to my workshop!"

"Hello, Poppy," the group chorused.

"I know you're all here because you love stories," Poppy went on. "And so do I! I thought I'd start our workshop by reading a couple of my very own stories to you." She selected a book from the pile and opened it. "This is the story of Sleeping Beauty. Once upon a time, many years ago..."

Rachel and Kirsty settled down to listen. But very soon it became clear that the story of Sleeping Beauty was completely wrong and *very* mixed-up. Princess Aurora pricked her finger on a knitting-needle, not a spinning-wheel, and she was only asleep for five years, not a hundred. Then, when the handsome prince woke the Sleeping Beauty with a kiss, she yawned and went back to sleep! All the children

23

laughed and Poppy, who'd been looking
increasingly bewildered as she read on,
hastily closed the book.

"Let's try another," she suggested,
picking up *Little Red Riding Hood*. But
only two pages in, as Little Red Riding
Hood walked through the woods to her
grandmother's house, the wolf pounced
on her and gobbled
her up. So that
was the end
of the story.
Poppy looked
very shocked
and confused
as the girls
glanced
sideways at each
other.

"Poor Poppy," Rachel whispered, "She doesn't know why all her stories are going so horribly wrong."

"But we do," Kirsty replied in a low voice. "This is all because Jack Frost's goblins have Libby the Story-Writing Fairy's magical object!"

"I think someone's playing a joke on me," Poppy murmured, shaking her head. She forced a smile. "OK, everyone, why don't we write a new story together? That'll be fun! Now, can anyone think of a character we can write about?"

There was silence. The girls racked their brains but simply couldn't think of a single idea.

"We could write about the park," a boy in the front row suggested.

"The park can be the setting for the story," Poppy explained gently, "But we need a *character*, someone who does something interesting."

This time there was an even longer silence. Then a squirrel scampered past, tail waving.

"Our character could be a squirrel," Poppy said, "What do you think? Has anyone got any plot ideas?"

"The squirrel could run up a tree," Rachel offered hesitantly.

"Good start," Poppy replied. "Why does the squirrel climb the tree? Is he looking for something?"

Everyone, including the girls, stared blankly at Poppy.

"My brain won't work!" Kirsty murmured, frustrated.

"He could be looking for another squirrel, I suppose," Poppy said with a shrug. "But it's not very exciting, is it?"

No one had anything to say and Poppy seemed to be out of ideas, too. The girls could see that the story-writing workshop was going from bad to worse.

"I'll let you write your own stories," Poppy said at last, and she began handing out pretty notebooks with painted silk covers. "Then you can read them out to each other." She gave Kirsty a pink notebook decorated with daisies and Rachel a blue one with a golden sun on the front.

"I can't think of a single thing to write," Rachel sighed. She laid her notebook on the rug and began rooting through her backpack for her pencil case. "This is going to be the most boring story ever!"

Kirsty took a pen from her pocket
and began scribbling down what they'd
just said about the squirrel. But then
her attention was caught by a very
faint glow hovering around Rachel's
notebook. Kirsty was puzzled. It seemed
almost like the painted sun was glowing
and shining with a magical golden light.

"Look, Rachel, fairy magic!" Kirsty
murmured in a low voice, nodding at the
notebook.

Quivering with excitement, but trying
not to show it, the girls moved to the
edge of the picnic rug where no one
else was sitting. Carefully Rachel
opened the notebook. A cloud of
shimmering sparkles tumbled out,
followed by a tiny fairy!

Super Scribe

"Remember me, girls?" the fairy whispered in her sweet, silvery voice, flicking back her rippling waves of golden hair. She was barefoot and wore a swishy, sea-green dress sparkling with silver stars. "I'm Libby the Story-Writing Fairy."

"Libby, you've arrived just in time," Kirsty told her. "Our story-writing is a total disaster!"

"We can't think of a single idea," Rachel added.

Libby frowned. "How terrible!" she sighed despairingly. She landed lightly on the rug, keeping out of sight behind Rachel and Kirsty. "I knew this was going to happen when Jack Frost stole my magical notebook.

We simply can't let him win, can we, girls? What would our human and fairy worlds be like without stories?"

"Awful!" the girls said together.

"I love good stories," Libby continued, "But stories will never turn out right again unless I find my magical notebook! You will help me, won't you, girls?"

Rachel and Kirsty nodded eagerly.

"We love stories, too," Rachel told the little fairy. "But I don't think there'll be many good ones today!" She glanced at the rest of the group. Everyone was staring blankly at their notebooks, and Libby and the girls could see that they'd hardly written anything. Poppy was walking around offering help and making suggestions, but she looked unhappy, too.

"Jack Frost has ruined everything!"
Libby said, very upset.

As Kirsty stared at the other children,
her eye fell on someone she hadn't
noticed so far. On the furthest corner
of one of the picnic rugs, separate from
every one else, sat a boy wearing a
floppy sunhat. He had a notebook on his
lap and he was bent over it, scribbling
away as fast as he could. As Kirsty
watched, he paused, read over what he'd
written and chuckled gleefully to himself.
Then he went on scribbling again.

"Rachel, look at that boy sitting over there, on his own," Kirsty whispered. "He seems to have *loads* of ideas. He can't stop writing!"

Rachel glanced over at the boy. At the same moment he happened to look up for just a fraction of a second, and Rachel instantly spotted a long, green nose under the peak of his hat.

"That's not a boy," she announced to Kirsty and Libby. "He's a goblin!"

"What shall we do?" Kirsty asked anxiously.

But before they could say anything more, Poppy also spotted the goblin writing away at top speed. Her face lit up and she hurried over to him.

"You seem to have a lot of ideas!" Poppy said with a smile. "How much have you written?"

"Pages and pages!" the goblin said proudly, flicking through his notebook. Rachel, Kirsty and Libby could see that he'd already filled almost half of it.

"Would you read your story to us?" Poppy asked, "We'd all love to hear it."

"It's not finished yet," the goblin mumbled gruffly.

"That doesn't matter," Poppy assured him. "Don't be shy! Stand up and let's hear it. What's it called?"

"It's called *The Greatest Goblin Who*

Ever Lived!" the goblin replied proudly. He climbed to his feet, cleared his throat and then held the notebook in front of him, ready to begin. As he did so, Libby let out a horrified gasp.

"Girls, I can see why that goblin is such a good writer," she declared indignantly. "It's because he has my magical notebook! We have to get it away from him. But I just don't know how!"

Thrilling Tale

Kirsty and Rachel looked more closely at the goblin's notebook. They could see it glowing very faintly with a golden haze of magic.

"Once upon a time," the goblin read out, "Jack Frost lived in a castle made of ice in the middle of a dark, snowy land. Jack Frost was grumpy and selfish and all he did every day was order his goblin servants around and make them do his bidding.

'Do this!' Jack Frost yelled. 'Do that! And hurry up about it!'

The goblins always tried their best, but Jack Frost was never satisfied.

'You idiots!' he would roar furiously, shooting bolts of ice at them from his magic wand. 'I'm fed up with the whole lot of you!'

Then the goblins would scurry around and try even harder to do exactly what Jack Frost wanted them to do, but their master was never happy.

So at last, one brave goblin decided to stand up for himself..."

As the goblin read on, Rachel, Kirsty and Libby exchanged amused glances. According to the author, the goblin in the story was cleverer, more handsome and more courageous than any other goblin, ever, and it was obvious that the goblin was writing about himself! However, when the goblin vividly described how his hero got the better of Jack Frost, pelting him with a flurry of huge snowballs until Jack Frost begged for mercy, everyone in the audience was spellbound, even Libby and the girls. The story was thrilling.

"And so the handsome, brave, intelligent goblin became Emperor of the Ice Castle," the goblin declared. "And he ruled over Jack Frost and the other goblins wisely and well. But behind the scenes, Jack Frost was plotting and planning dark deeds! He was determined to regain his Ice Throne and rule the kingdom once more..."

The goblin stopped reading and everyone broke into applause.

"That was wonderful!" Poppy gasped, "So imaginative!"

"Tell us what happens next," begged one of the girls, but the goblin shook his head.

"I haven't finished the story yet," he retorted, and the audience groaned with disappointment.

"The goblin's story is a big hit," Libby whispered to Rachel and Kirsty. "But it's the magic of my notebook that's turned him into a wonderful author!"

"Can't you write the rest of it now?" Poppy asked the goblin. "Everyone is longing to hear what Jack Frost does next. He's a wonderful character, a real baddie!"

"It's lucky for you that Jack Frost isn't here!" another boy called. He was sitting at the back and was wearing a bright green baseball cap. "Otherwise you'd be in *big* trouble!"

Rachel could see the goblin looked rather nervous when he heard that.

"We'll take a break and have some juice and biscuits," Poppy announced, smiling at the goblin. "That will give you time to write more of your extraordinary story!"

"Maybe we should try and get the notebook back now?" Kirsty suggested quietly to Rachel and Libby. "I've thought of something that might work."

"Yes, go for it!" Libby agreed eagerly. She tucked herself neatly away inside Rachel's pencil case, and then the girls went over to the goblin. He had seated himself on the picnic rug again, preparing to write another chapter.

"Your story really is brilliant!" Kirsty told him.

"I know," the goblin said happily, preening himself.

"We'd really like to read it again," Kirsty went on. "Would you swap notebooks with me? You can read my story about a squirrel, although it's not half as good as yours."

The goblin stared suspiciously at them. Then he gave a squeal of rage. "I can see that fairy hiding in your pencil case!" he hissed at Rachel. "Leave me alone!"

And, clutching the notebook tightly to his chest, he jumped up and raced off.

"Sorry, girls, he spotted me peeping out!" Libby gasped.

"Don't worry, Libby," Rachel assured her, "We'll catch him!" And she and Kirsty chased after the goblin.

Some of the other children noticed the goblin running off and they followed too, shouting, "Come back! We want to hear the rest of your story!"

The goblin charged across the
playground, dodging around the
swings and the sandpit. Then, to the
girls' dismay, he seemed to vanish.
But suddenly Rachel
spotted him
clambering
up a tree in
the distance,
just before he
disappeared into
the topmost
branches.
Quickly Libby
and the girls
ran after him.

"Where's that boy gone?" asked
one of the other children, everyone
looking very disappointed when they

couldn't see the goblin anywhere. After
a few minutes they all gave up and
returned to the workshop. Meanwhile
Kirsty and Rachel slipped behind the tree
out of sight.

"Fairies can't climb, but they *can* fly!"
Libby murmured, smiling. With one
swish of her wand, Rachel and Kirsty
were instantly transformed into tiny,
sparkly-winged fairies. Then together

they all flew up into the tree.

The goblin was sitting on a branch, still gripping the notebook. He shrieked with angry surprise as Libby and the girls appeared, and began edging warily away from them along the branch.

"Go away!" the goblin roared.

"Let's try and get the notebook," Libby whispered to the girls. "But we'll have to be careful the goblin doesn't fall out of the tree!"

The three of them took it in turns to swoop down, trying to grab the notebook, but the goblin kept swatting them away with his free hand. Then Kirsty had an idea. Instead of flying down from above, she flew *underneath* the branch and popped up right in front of the goblin.

"Aaargh!" the goblin screamed, throwing up his hands in fright. He dropped the magical notebook and Rachel and Libby raced to catch it. But they were just a fraction too late. The notebook tumbled downwards.

Suddenly the boy from the workshop, in the green baseball cap, appeared under the tree. He caught the notebook neatly and glanced up to see where it had come from. Kirsty's heart sank as she saw a long, green nose underneath

the baseball cap.

"It's another goblin!" she shouted.
"And he has the magical notebook!"

Success Story

"Now it's *my* turn to write a story in the magical notebook!" the goblin cried in glee. Waving the notebook triumphantly aloft, he skipped off towards the playground. Libby, Rachel and Kirsty groaned in dismay.

"After him, girls!" Libby yelled. Leaving the other goblin climbing sulkily down the tree, the three fairy friends whizzed off.

When Libby, Rachel and Kirsty
caught up with the goblin in the baseball
cap, they found him perched on the
climbing frame.
He was scribbling
frantically in the
magical notebook,
murmuring the
words aloud to
himself.

"The goblin in
the baseball cap
raced up to the
battlements of the
Ice Castle where he found the goblin
emperor waiting for him.

'Now we'll see who's the most
handsome, clever and brave goblin of
them all!' the goblin in the cap cried."

As the goblin continued his story, telling how the two goblins fought an exciting duel, some of the other children from the story workshop hurried over to listen.

"We'll have to wait until everyone's gone before we try to get the notebook," Libby whispered, beckoning to the girls to hide behind one of the slides.

Rachel nodded. But she couldn't help noticing how entranced the goblin's audience were with his story, and suddenly an idea popped into her head. Quickly she whispered it to Kirsty and Libby.

"You want me to disguise you as Crafts Week judges?" Libby raised her eyebrows. "Of course I can do that!"

Libby swished her wand above Kirsty

and Rachel, and glittery fairy sparkles
fell softly around them. When the mist
of magic cleared, the girls stared at each
other in surprise. Kirsty now wore a pair
of glasses and her hair was tied up in a
ponytail, while Rachel wore a large sun
hat with the brim pulled down low. Both
of them were wearing pretty floral-print
dresses instead
of their T-shirts
and shorts.

   "Good luck!"
Libby whispered,
sliding into
the pocket of
Kirsty's dress.
Then the girls
hurried out from
behind the slide.

The goblin was just finishing his story. "And the goblin in the baseball cap became the new Emperor of the Ice Castle!" he announced. "And his powerful magic changed his baseball cap into a golden crown, set with sparkling green emeralds…"

As the children applauded, Kirsty and Rachel strode through the audience towards the goblin.

"Your story was wonderful!" Kirsty
told the goblin. "My friend and I are
Crafts Week judges, and your story is so
good, we want everyone, everywhere, to
read it!"

"Hurrah!" the goblin cheered happily,
waving the magical notebook around his
head in excitement.

"We want to turn your story into a book that will be in every bookshop and library in the whole world," Rachel said as the other children began to drift away, back to the workshop.

"So to do that, we'll need your notebook," Kirsty added, holding out her hand. She tried not to look too eager. Would the goblin agree – or would he guess what they were up to?

Happy Ending

"Sure!" the goblin agreed immediately, and he handed the magical notebook to Kirsty. Both girls breathed heartfelt sighs of relief, and Libby zoomed out of Kirsty's pocket.

"Give that back, you pesky fairy!" the goblin screeched furiously as Libby took possession of her precious notebook.

As the notebook shrank, in a cloud of sparkling magic, to its Fairyland size, the goblin who'd been up the tree came dashing over to the climbing-frame.

"You lost the notebook, you idiot!" he yelled, glaring at the other goblin.

"Don't call me an idiot," the second goblin shouted, "My story was a million times more exciting than yours!"

Libby winked at the girls and quickly waved her wand. There was a burst of sparkling fairy dust, and both goblins looked extremely surprised to find that each of them was holding a book bound in bright green leather with gold writing on the cover.

"Now you each have a copy of your own story," Libby said with a smile.

The goblins looked thrilled.

"I'll read you my story," the first goblin said to the other as they trudged off across the park.

"No, I'll read you *my* story!" the other one snapped back.

As the goblins wandered off into the distance, still arguing, Libby turned to

Rachel and Kirsty. "Girls, our story today will have a very happy ending, after all, thanks to you!" She smiled. "I can't tell you how grateful I am. Your friendship and loyalty mean so much to all of us in Fairyland." Then, with one flick of her wand, Libby's magic swept away the girls' disguises, returning them to normal. "Now go and enjoy the rest of your story-writing workshop," Libby said. "And I'll see you very soon!" And with a wave, she vanished.

When Kirsty and Rachel rejoined the workshop, they could already see a difference. All the children were writing in their notebooks, brows furrowed in concentration, and Poppy, too, was looking much happier as she moved around offering advice.

"I feel like I'm bursting with ideas now!" Kirsty remarked, flipping open her notebook. "I've thought of a fantastic woodland adventure for my squirrel."

"I'm going to finish the story about the Rainbow Fairies we started earlier," Rachel decided. "I can remember everything that happened now!"

The girls began to write, and soon they were absorbed in their stories, scribbling away and  occasionally stopping to read bits out to each other.

"You're working very hard!" Poppy commented, coming over to them. "May I see what you've written?"

A little shyly, Rachel handed over her notebook. Poppy read through it.

"Rachel, this story is wonderfully creative!" Poppy declared with a smile.

"I love your seven fairy characters, particularly Ruby the Red Fairy. You've made them so real, they could almost fly off the page!"

"Thank you, Poppy," Rachel said proudly.

"I think you should enter this in the Crafts Week competition," Poppy went on, handing the notebook back to Rachel.

"That's brilliant, Rachel!" Kirsty exclaimed happily. "Now we'll *both* have an entry in the competition tomorrow."

Poppy clapped her hands to get everyone's attention. "I'm afraid the workshop is coming to an end," she announced, "I do hope you've enjoyed it. And to finish off, I have some signed copies for you of my latest book. It's called *A Rainspell Island Fairytale*."

Kirsty and Rachel grinned at each other. Even Poppy Fields, the famous

author, didn't know about their secret
fairy friends!

The End

Now it's time for Kirsty and
Rachel to help...

Roxie the Baking Fairy

Read on for a sneak peek...

"I'm really sad it's the last day of our holiday," Kirsty sighed, placing a pile of folded t-shirts in her suitcase. "But I'm super-excited about the Crafts Week exhibition and competition!"

"So am I," Rachel agreed. The girls were in Kirsty's attic bedroom at the B&B, packing their things ready to go home that evening. They'd spent their week's holiday on Rainspell Island staying one night at the B&B with Mr and Mrs Tate, and the next at the campsite with Rachel's parents.

"It's been brilliant fun having a

go at all the different crafts, hasn't it?" said Kirsty enthusiastically, and Rachel nodded. It was Crafts Week on Rainspell, and for the past six days the girls had attended various workshops. Today there was an exhibition of the best crafts produced during the week, and prizes would be awarded.

Read **Roxie the Baking Fairy** to find out what adventures are in store for Kirsty and Rachel!

Join in the magic online by signing up to the Rainbow Magic fan club!

Sign up today at:
www.rainbowmagicbooks.co.uk

Meet the
Magical Crafts Fairies

Jack Frost has stolen the Magical Crafts Fairies' special objects. Can Kirsty and Rachel help get them back before Rainspell Island's Crafts Week is ruined?

www.rainbowmagicbooks.co.uk

Competition!

The Magical Crafts Fairies have created a special
competition just for you!
In the back of each book in the Magical Crafts series there
will be a question for you to answer.
First you need to collect the answer from the back
of each book in the series.
Once you have all the answers, take the first letter from
each one and arrange them to spell a secret word!
When you have the answer, go online and enter!

What is Libby the Story-Writing Fairy's magical object?

_ _ _ _ _ _ _

We will put all the correct entries into a draw and select
a winner to receive a special Rainbow Magic Goody Bag
featuring lots of treats for you and your fairy friends.
You'll also star in a new Rainbow Magic story!

Enter online now at www.rainbowmagicbooks.co.uk

No purchase required. Only one entry per child. Two prize draws will take place on 29th August
2014 and 31st October 2014. Alternatively readers can send the answer on a postcard to:
Rainbow Magic, Magical Crafts Fairies Competition,
Orchard Books, 338 Euston Road, London, NW1 3BH. Australian readers can write to:
Rainbow Magic, Magical Crafts Fairies Competition, Hachette Children's Books,
level 17/207 Kent St, Sydney, NSW 2000. E-mail: childrens.books@hachette.com.au.
New Zealand readers should write to:
Rainbow Magic, Magical Crafts Fairies Competition,
PO Box 3255, Shortland St, Auckland 1140

Have you read them all?

The Rainbow Fairies

1. Ruby the Red Fairy ☐
2. Amber the Orange Fairy ☐
3. Saffron the Yellow Fairy ☐
4. Fern the Green Fairy ☐
5. Sky the Blue Fairy ☐
6. Izzy the Indigo Fairy ☐
7. Heather the Violet Fairy ☐

The Weather Fairies

8. Crystal the Snow Fairy ☐
9. Abigail the Breeze Fairy ☐
10. Pearl the Cloud Fairy ☐
11. Goldie the Sunshine Fairy ☐
12. Evie the Mist Fairy ☐
13. Storm the Lightning Fairy ☐
14. Hayley the Rain Fairy ☐

The Party Fairies

15. Cherry the Cake Fairy ☐
16. Melodie the Music Fairy ☐
17. Grace the Glitter Fairy ☐
18. Honey the Sweet Fairy ☐
19. Polly the Party Fun Fairy ☐
20. Phoebe the Fashion Fairy ☐
21. Jasmine the Present Fairy ☐

The Jewel Fairies

22. India the Moonstone Fairy ☐
23. Scarlett the Garnet Fairy ☐
24. Emily the Emerald Fairy ☐
25. Chloe the Topaz Fairy ☐
26. Amy the Amethyst Fairy ☐
27. Sophie the Sapphire Fairy ☐
28. Lucy the Diamond Fairy ☐

The Pet Keeper Fairies

29. Katie the Kitten Fairy ☐
30. Bella the Bunny Fairy ☐
31. Georgia the Guinea Pig Fairy ☐
32. Lauren the Puppy Fairy ☐
33. Harriet the Hamster Fairy ☐
34. Molly the Goldfish Fairy ☐
35. Penny the Pony Fairy ☐

The Fun Day Fairies

36. Megan the Monday Fairy ☐
37. Tallulah the Tuesday Fairy ☐
38. Willow the Wednesday Fairy ☐
39. Thea the Thursday Fairy ☐
40. Freya the Friday Fairy ☐
41. Sienna the Saturday Fairy ☐
42. Sarah the Sunday Fairy ☐

The Petal Fairies

43. Tia the Tulip Fairy ☐
44. Pippa the Poppy Fairy ☐
45. Louise the Lily Fairy ☐
46. Charlotte the Sunflower Fairy ☐
47. Olivia the Orchid Fairy ☐
48. Danielle the Daisy Fairy ☐
49. Ella the Rose Fairy ☐

The Dance Fairies
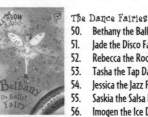
50. Bethany the Ballet Fairy ☐
51. Jade the Disco Fairy ☐
52. Rebecca the Rock'n'Roll Fairy ☐
53. Tasha the Tap Dance Fairy ☐
54. Jessica the Jazz Fairy ☐
55. Saskia the Salsa Fairy ☐
56. Imogen the Ice Dance Fairy ☐

The Sporty Fairies

57. Helena the Horseriding Fairy ☐
58. Francesca the Football Fairy ☐
59. Zoe the Skating Fairy ☐
60. Naomi the Netball Fairy ☐
61. Samantha the Swimming Fairy ☐
62. Alice the Tennis Fairy ☐
63. Gemma the Gymnastics Fairy ☐

The Music Fairies

64. Poppy the Piano Fairy ☐
65. Ellie the Guitar Fairy ☐
66. Fiona the Flute Fairy ☐
67. Danni the Drum Fairy ☐
68. Maya the Harp Fairy ☐
69. Victoria the Violin Fairy ☐
70. Sadie the Saxophone Fairy ☐

The Magical Animal Fairies

71. Ashley the Dragon Fairy ☐
72. Lara the Black Cat Fairy ☐
73. Erin the Firebird Fairy ☐
74. Rihanna the Seahorse Fairy ☐
75. Sophia the Snow Swan Fairy ☐
76. Leona the Unicorn Fairy ☐
77. Caitlin the Ice Bear Fairy ☐

The Green Fairies

78. Nicole the Beach Fairy ☐
79. Isabella the Air Fairy ☐
80. Edie the Garden Fairy ☐
81. Coral the Reef Fairy ☐
82. Lily the Rainforest Fairy ☐
83. Carrie the Snow Cap Fairy ☐
84. Milly the River Fairy ☐

The Ocean Fairies

85. Ally the Dolphin Fairy ☐
86. Amelie the Seal Fairy ☐
87. Pia the Penguin Fairy ☐
88. Tess the Sea Turtle Fairy ☐
89. Stephanie the Starfish Fairy ☐
90. Whitney the Whale Fairy ☐
91. Courtney the Clownfish Fairy ☐

The Twilight Fairies

92. Ava the Sunset Fairy ☐
93. Lexi the Firefly Fairy ☐
94. Zara the Starlight Fairy ☐
95. Morgan the Midnight Fairy ☐
96. Yasmin the Night Owl Fairy ☐
97. Maisie the Moonbeam Fairy ☐
98. Sabrina the Sweet Dreams Fairy ☐

The Showtime Fairies

99. Madison the Magic Show Fairy ☐
100. Leah the Theatre Fairy ☐
101. Alesha the Acrobat Fairy ☐
102. Darcey the Dance Diva Fairy ☐
103. Taylor the Talent Show Fairy ☐
104. Amelia the Singing Fairy ☐
105. Isla the Ice Star Fairy ☐

The Princess Fairies

106. Honor the Happy Days Fairy ☐
107. Demi the Dressing-Up Fairy ☐
108. Anya the Cuddly Creatures Fairy ☐
109. Elisa the Adventure Fairy ☐
110. Lizzie the Sweet Treats Fairy ☐
111. Maddie the Playtime Fairy ☐
112. Eva the Enchanted Ball Fairy ☐

The Pop Star Fairies

113. Jessie the Lyrics Fairy ☐
114. Adele the Singing Coach Fairy ☐
115. Vanessa the Dance Steps Fairy ☐
116. Miley the Stylist Fairy ☐
117. Frankie the Make-Up Fairy ☐
118. Rochelle the Star Spotter Fairy ☐
119. Una the Concert Fairy ☐

The Fashion Fairies

120. Miranda the Beauty Fairy ☐
121. Claudia the Accessories Fairy ☐
122. Tyra the Dress Designer Fairy ☐
123. Alexa the Fashion Reporter Fairy ☐
124. Matilda the Hair Stylist Fairy ☐
125. Brooke the Photographer Fairy ☐
126. Lola the Fashion Fairy ☐

The Sweet Fairies

127. Lottie the Lollipop Fairy ☐
128. Esme the Ice Cream Fairy ☐
129. Coco the Cupcake Fairy ☐
130. Clara the Chocolate Fairy ☐
131. Madeleine the Cookie Fairy ☐
132. Layla the Candyfloss Fairy ☐
133. Nina the Birthday Cake Fairy ☐

The Baby Animal Rescue Fairies

134. Mae the Panda Fairy ☐
135. Kitty the Tiger Fairy ☐
136. Mara the Meerkat Fairy ☐
137. Savannah the Zebra Fairy ☐
138. Kimberley the Koala Fairy ☐
139. Rosie the Honey Bear Fairy ☐
140. Anna the Arctic Fox Fairy ☐

The Magical Crafts Fairies

141. Kayla the Pottery Fairy ☐
142. Annabelle the Drawing Fairy ☐
143. Zadie the Sewing Fairy ☐
144. Josie the Jewellery-Making Fairy ☐
145. Violet the Painting Fairy ☐
146. Libby the Story-Writing Fairy ☐
147. Roxie the Baking Fairy ☐

There's a book of fairy fun for everyone!

www.rainbowmagicbooks.co.uk

Lila & Myla the Twins Fairies

Meet Lila and Myla the Twins Fairies!
Can the fairies stop Jack Frost before he uses
their magic to create his very own twin?

www.rainbowmagicbooks.co.uk